AF350568

BEDTIME FANTASIES

- Ajaydeep M.

Copyright © 2021

A Friend's Betrayal

The door bell rings and I was getting more nervous as I was rushing to finish getting ready for my date. His name was Marcus and he ran some businesses with his best friend. I quickly finished my look with red lace bodysuit dress with a pair of black heels to match. The bell rang for the second time and I quickly ran to open the door.

"Hi love, you look stunning as ever" Marcus said.

"And you look as handsome as ever" I have to admit it he looked good wearing a black tuxedo with his gray eyes that matches with his brushed up black hair. Oh god what a perfect guy.

Let's go? He asked.

And I quickly said "Yes" he led the way on his black Lamborghini. Should I be proud? Of course, his rich and handsome.

As I was walking I teased him and lead his hands on the way on my butt cheek. He was surprised to feel that I wasn't wearing any underwear. Well, I am always ready.

He opens the door for me. What a gentleman he is. After I got inside, he closed the door and he walks to the other side and we drove off on the way to the yacht.

"So what did you do all day?" He asks

"I just slept all day, tired of what happens to us yesterday" he laughed on what I said.

"This will be a tiring night again love" Marcus said.

"I'm always ready" and winked at him. He chuckles. After a few minutes of driving, we arrived at the yacht. There was a guy waiting for us.

"Sir Marcus Clarkson?" The guy asked. Marcus nodded and the guy lead us on a beautiful yacht. The yacht started to move and we are about to eat when Marcus slide his fingers on my pussy...

"Ooohh" I moaned when his finger slides on my hole. He was teasing me and I like it.

"Faster please" and he obeys me and finger fucks my pussy. He pushed in and out like there was no tomorrow.

"Ughh love, make me cum" He was about to add one more finger inside me when the waiter started giving us our food. Marcus removes his fingers inside me. He licks his fingers and look at me intensely. After we finish our food, he led me inside the yacht on the way to our room.

As soon as we reach the door, Marcus started kissing me roughly. I moaned as he kisses me. His hands travel on my boobs and massaged my nipples and he groan. Hearing him groan makes my pussy so wet and crave for more. His hands travel on my back to unzip my dress he started to undress me. My dress falls down on the floor. He looked at me intently and his hands touches my womanhood. He slowly rubs my clit and my entrance. I moaned and leaned my head on the wall.

"Oh god Marcus, I can't take it anymore fuck me please" I moaned.

"Not yet love" He said and pushed two fingers inside me and finger fucks me hard.

"Yes love moan for me you're so fucking wet. I am good at making you wet don't I? He groans at my ear.

"Ugh yes love you are good and I want you to fuck me now" I said while his fingers are still busy in and out on my wet pussy. I try to absorb all the pleasure that I am feeling but his thumb reaches for my clit and do circles around. I can't help but to scream for the pleasure.

I grab his head and pushed him for a kiss, I bite his lower lip and as he groans I released one loud moan and I release my juices.

"I love to make you cum. Now get ready cause I'll be fucking you nonstop tonight." He says and started unbuttoning his tuxedo. He placed my hands on his growing erection. I gently rub it making him begs for more.

He guided my head to his erection and said "I want you to fuck with your mouth Anna" I opened my mouth and slide his erection on my mouth. I licked the tip of it and tasted his pre-cum. he pushed my head all the way down I gave him a deepthroat and he groans loudly.

"Oh god you are so good at sucking my cock" he said. It was like a music on my ears so I suck his cock up and down faster. His expression becomes more intense.

"You like my big cock, don't you?" He lifts my head up and pushes me on the bed. He kisses my legs up to thighs.

"Marcus please" I begged.

"All in good time love" He says and dips his head on my vagina. His tongue makes contacts with my clit.

"Oh god Marcus" I moaned as I leaned my head on the bed making my body arched. I am shaking right now and he laps up the juices that are pouring out of me at this point I know that I was about to cum. He sticks out his tongue and licks my clit. His tongue feels so good. I was near when he stops and ask me.

"Are you okay? You're shaking violently" while looking at me.

"I'm okay don't stop"

He gets back to it and added two fingers inside me while eating my pussy. I was climbing and climbing and I'm there.

"OH MY GOD, YES I NEED YOU NOW!" I said and pushed him back and now he is now under me. I grab his dick and slowly rub my pussy into it.

"Ride me baby"

I was teasing him when he grabs his cock and in one swift move, he is now inside me.

"Oh fuck love your pussy is so tight" he says while he clenched his teeth.

I throw my head in euphoria while I was riding him. Watching him fall apart under me is so sexy so I switched back our positions he is now on top of me.

He continues to thrust deep into me at a slow and gentle pace. His mouth whispers.

"Faster, Harder Marcus please" I beg.

"Someone's being greedy. Beg for it love. Beg for me to do fuck you harder."

I groan and he stills inside me. "NO!"

"I said beg Anna"

"FUCK ME MARCUS PLEASE I WANT YOUR BIG COCK TO FUCK MY PUSSY HARDER"

"Your wish is my command love" He says and thrust into me so hard that I screamed.

"Scream my name love"

"Come on love I want to hear you scream my name"

"Mar... cus.. Mar.. AHHHH!"I tried to scream his name but I failed it comes out to be a garbled moans.

"SAY IT LOVE" He yells and thrust into me deeper and way harder which made me loose my mind and I know that I was about to come. I let go and scream his name.

"OH MY GOD MARCUS" I gasped and my legs are shaking.

"I am not yet done love" and thrusts more even though I just finished coming. After a few minutes of him fucking me. He came inside me and we slept.

On the next day, I was walking through the mall when I bumped into Lucas, he was Marcus's best friend and I can't lie Lucas got some looks too. All woman who are walking pass through us is eyeing on this man.

"Hi Anna! I see that you are alone probably Marcus is busy with our business huh? He said.

"Yeah, right Lucky Boy!" I commented.

"Mind joining you for today? I have nothing to do" I nodded as a response and we stroll through the mall. As we are walking through the Bookstore my phone suddenly beeped. It was a text from Marcus saying that he is already outside the mall to pick me up. It's already 8pm sh*t I forgot the time.

"Is there any problem Anna?" Marcus asked.

"Uh nothing, Marcus is already outside waiting for me"

"Okay, come on let's go." we are now walking towards Marcus's car and I can see that he is looking right into my eyes telling me that I have done something wrong.

"What's up bro? I bumped into Anna a while ago and I thought of I should accompany her since she is alone" Lucas said.

"I'm fine bro do you want to come into our house? Let's drink." Marcus requested. Lucas agreed on going into our house and as we drove on the way home Marcus is not talking to me. I wonder what did I do wrong to make him angry?

When we got home. I take a quick shower and put on my usual clothes my lingerie. I can hear Marcus and Lucas talking they are laughing about something and I got curious so I walked outside and they are already drunk. I greet the both of them. They turn their heads and looked at me up and down and they both looked at each other. I sense that something is not right so I took a step backwards.

"Come here my love" Marcus spoke.

"Anna can you accompany us" Lucas said. They both ask at the same time. When I was near our bedroom's door, they quickly ran and held my arms.

"MARCUS LUCAS LET GO OF ME!"

"Shhhh, this will be exciting" Marcus whispered. And I know that something wrong will be happening tonight. Oh god help me please... They held me tightly and they are walking us through the basement. I have never been in here since Marcus wouldn't let me step on this basement.

It was dark in here; Lucas let's go of my arm and he opens the little bulb. As soon as the room lights up, I saw a bed in the middle also there is a mini sofa and cabinets that I don't know what is inside.

"Let's play a game my love" Marcus suggested.

"You're going to love it" Marcus added. I am getting more nervous of what's going to happen. Should I scream? There is no one who can hear me since our house is far from the other houses.

"Do you want to know our secrets, Lil Anna?" Lucas suddenly asked.

"What secrets Lucas? Are you hiding things from me?" I looked at Marcus and he looks back and he chuckles.

"You know love, you don't know a single thing from us. You only know lies not the truth" Okay... Things are getting out of my hand and I don't like what I am feeling right now. I was about to leave the basement room when Marcus grabbed my hair from behind and dragged me harshly leading me to the bed.

"OUCH MARCUS STOP YOU'RE HURTING ME" I yell. Marcus didn't respond as if he doesn't hear me.

"Lucas, get the cuffs" Marcus said.

"What are you going to do Marcus?" I asked. And again, he didn't bother responding he didn't even look at me. Marcus is still grabbing my hair tightly and it hurt so bad.

Lucas was holding four cuffs and smirking while walking towards us. Marcus grabs my hand and cuff me in one of the sides of the bed. I was resisting but they are two of them and they are much stronger than I am.

Both my hands are cuffed as well as my feet. Lucas was holding a scissors and he whispers something to Marcus and Marcus just laughed and said "Go, you fucker". It was like a go signal for Lucas. Lucas started walking towards me.

"Marcus, Lucas please let me go" I beg. They didn't listen. Lucas was just walking towards me. I was so scared right now of what's going to happen. Lucas was now in front of me. He holds the end of my lingerie and cuts it off in the middle exposing my body in front of him.

"Fuck Marcus you tasted this body first? Damn you're so lucky you bastard!"

"No please Lucas let me go. I don't want this" I cried. Lucas started massaging my nipples, I cried loudly as he licks my right boobs while his hand is playing with the other. I tried to move left and right so that he can't properly do what his doing when he stop... and slapped me.

I winced in pain and tears are running down on my face.

"Bitch try to move again and I'll make you suffer" Lucas said. I didn't move and let him do what he wants. When he is tired of playing with my boobs, his hands travel down to my womanhood. He started caressing my clit.

"Marcus, can you pass me some of our intense toys?" Marcus walks down to the cabinet and I saw a lot of dildo's, vibrators, and things that are for sex. Marcus gives Lucas a white thing that looks a vibrator. He clicks it and it vibrates he puts it on my clit and I gasped.

"OHHH" I moaned. On the sudden vibrate. My pussy hasn't recovered yet when he increased the intensity. My body is getting shivers on the pleasure that I was getting.

"OH MY FUCKING GOD" I moaned. I am near. My body is convulsing I need to release my fcking juices. Damn this feels so good. I don't care if this is right or wrong what matters is I am about to come.

"More please, I want more" I said.

"We are just getting started Anna" Lucas said and he stops the vibrator. I was about to protest when he suddenly inserts two fingers inside me. His fingers thrust and thrust faster and harder.

"THAT'S IT LUCAS MORE PLEASE FUCK ME" I yell from the pleasure. One last thrust and I release my juices. Lucas removes his fingers inside me. He removes his pants and gets on top of me. He thrusts his cock inside of me.

"Damn so tight Anna" He groans.

"Fuck me harder" I whispered on his ear.

We were having our moment when Marcus interrupted and said "Mind if I join you guys?"

"Can you please remove the cuffs..." I asked them. And they released both of my arms and feet. Marcus grabs my hair and makes me kneel in front of him.

"Suck it" Marcus said. I touched his crotched and suck it all in one go. He groans loudly. He tightened his grip on my hair and push me up and down. Lucas grabbed my ass and positioned himself on my back and thrusted his cock inside me and he began fucking me.

"AHHH, yes Lucas fuck me harder! Give it all to me! AHHH YES YES!" I yelled.

Marcus roughly fucks my mouth, that I started gaggling on his cock but he doesn't stop not until I nearly passed out.

Lucas guided me on top him and Marcus positioned himself on top of me... They are planning to enter both of my holes at the same time.

As soon as they both enter me, I feel both pleasure and pain. Lucas fucks me like his cock was about destroy my pussy. Marcus is fucking my butt hole harder than usual.

"Oh gooddd!! I can't take this anymore. I am going to cum!" I said. They both increase their speed they fuck me faster and harder and fck my body is shaking intensely.

"I am cumming!" I push my pussy up and about to release my juices when I squirted in front of Lucas's face. I squirted and lie downs on the side of the bed while my legs are still shaking.

They take turns on fucking my pussy until they reached their orgasms. After that night I saw Lucas and Marcus leaving the basement and I fell asleep.

I woke up the next day, and I found out that Lucas and Marcus are gone for a bit. There is a sticky note on the refrigerator "Hi Anna, we will be gone for a few minutes or hours it depends. We had fun last night. Wear something sexy. We have a surprise for you" I smiled and hurriedly take a bath. And wore a body con dress with a long slit on the side.

I was at the kitchen cooking when I hear a car engine outside. It must be Lucas and Marcus. I walked towards the entrance and opened the door for them.

"Hello Anna, are you excited about your surprise?" Lucas asked.

"Later Lucas, let's eat first. What do we have for dinner?" Marcus replied.

"Oh, I cooked some beef broccoli since we are almost out of food stocks" while we were eating Lucas and Marcus are talking about business and I just continued eating. After we eat, Marcus and Lucas started talking about important things.

"Anna, open it it's for you" Lucas said. I opened the paper bag and I saw a black panty and a remote control. Oh I know what is this.

"Do you like it? Try it." Marcus said. I removed the panty that I was wearing and replaced it with the vibrator panty. Marcus and Lucas was watching me wear it.

"Give it to me" Marcus said. I gave him the remote and he started pressing the remote at Level 1.

"Uhhh, more Marcus" I moaned. This vibrator panty was so good that my pussy becomes wet. Lucas walked towards me.

"FUCK" I moaned as he kisses my neck. He removed the panty and pushed me through the sofa.

"OH HOLY FUCK" I screamed when he reaches my clit and circling his fingers feeling my wetness.

"You're this horny huh" Lucas whispered.

"FUCK LUCAS! YOU'RE SO GOOD" I moaned as he penetrates his fingers inside me. His kisses travels down to my boobs. He sucked it like he was a hungry baby. I let out a soft moan as he bites my nipples. I want to be fucked now.

"Lucas fuck me please" He continued on going in and out of my pussy. I can feel that his fingers are filled with my wetness. His thumb played with my sensitive clit. Making me scream louder.

"UGHHHH MY GOD LUCASSS!"

I can feel that my body was about to give up, my legs are shaking and I know that I was about to come.

"YES Lucas, Fuck me please I am about to come. FASTER!" I moaned Lucas is still sucking my breast and his fingers is still thrusting my little pussy.

"I am cumming" I said. Lucas stopped his fingers on entering me.

"Why did you stop?"

"You will not cum until I say so" He begin thrusting his two long fingers inside me slowly hitting my most sensitive part. I looked at him and beg him to make me cum.

"Please let me cum" He stopped. And placed my legs around his neck and he entered me whole without any warnings.

"OH GOD" I moaned. His cock is big that my hole are swollen from what we did last night but he doesn't care and fucks me like a mad man.

"Shit Anna you're so tight" He moaned as he goes deeper and harder inside me. It feels so good.

"Lucas slower, slower please go slower" I screamed but instead he goes faster and faster and he plays with my clit.

I feel like my body is being destroyed if he doesn't go slower. He bend and look at my eyes. I can see that his eyes was full of lust.

His fingers are playing with my clit and he is thrusting really fast. Minutes have passed Lucas began thrusting more faster and more deeper than a while ago.

"I AM COMING LUCAS!" He removes his erection inside me. I moaned as he removes it inside me. His full and long and I don't know how did I able to take his shaft.

"Not yet Anna, not yet" He lifted me and moves me down on the table. I was facing the table. He pushed my half body so my front body was lying on the table.

"OUCHH!" I yell as he slapped my butt. He slapped it for a few times and later on caressed it.

"You're so sexy Anna, You can cum whenever you want now" and I felt that he penetrated me from behind. He lunge inside me so I can't control my moan.

"UGH UHHH" one after another moan, He thrust it faster and faster. If he was rough earlier this one was a lot rougher. He grabbed my hair.

"Do you like it Anna?" He asked. I moaned as a response. He reached for my clit and his fingers circles around it. I am completely lost from the pleasure right now.

"YES LUCAS! AH! AH!" I screamed.

"I'm close" He said and thrust deeper and harder. I know I was close too.

"I"M CUMMING" after a few more thrust. I felt his hot juices inside me.

Marcus only watched us from the other side of the sofa.

"Let's wash you up" Marcus said and carried me to our room.

He puts me down on our bathroom. He opened the shower. He pulls me on the bathtub. He started putting soap on my body. I never knew what kind of man I loved. I never know what is behind all of this. I understand Marcus and Lucas and I forgive them no matter what.

Marcus washed my pussy, I moaned as he touches it. He looks at me and washed my body. He pushed me on the corner and lifts my right leg. His penis entered my pussy. OH GOD I missed this.

Marcus's POV

Fuck, I can't control myself. She was so good at making me hard. Shit this pussy was so good, from all of the woman that I fucked she was the best one that's why I am keeping her.

"UGH fuck you" I groaned. As I continue to fuck her. Her pussy was so tight even though Lucas just fucked her. I reached for her nipples while I was still banging her. She closed her eyes and feels the pleasure that I was giving to her. I pinched her pink nipples. She opened her eyes and winced.

"AWW" she lets a small noise. She's sexy. I need to do this quick. We still have plans for her. This was the last time she'll feel this before everything happens.

I used my hands to choke her. I can't do it anymore she feels so damn good. Fuck that pussy I will missed this. I fucked her faster and deeper.

"SHIT MARCUS" she moaned. I love to hear you moan Anna. I can feel her vaginal walls started getting tight on my crotch. I know that she was about to cum. So I fucked her faster. I can hear my balls slapping her ass. I felt that it was more wet because she releases her juices that's why I continued to fucked her. God this feels so damn good.

I stabbed her a few more times, and I know I was about to come so I withdraw my shaft from her and make her kneel in front of me. I let her suck my dick.

"Your mouth was the best" I groaned as she puts my dick in her mouth. I pushed my dick hard on her mouth as she chokes. It felt amazing watching her struggling with my crotch in her mouth. After one hard thrust, I released my juices in her mouth.

We cleanse ourselves. We got out the bathroom and I checked the wall clock. It was 11:30pm. My phone suddenly rang but before I answered it.

"Anna, we are going somewhere" I said. And answered the phone. It was Lucas calling.

"Are you guys ready" Lucas asked.

"Yeah, give us five minutes" I said and ended the call.

"Where are we going Marcus?" Anna answered but I didn't bother answering

"Here drink this first before we go"

ANNA's POV

I woke up and my head hurts. Where am I? Where is Marcus and Lucas? I am at a hall. Tied in a chair. What's going on? Are they going to abandon me? I'm scared.

I was scanning and looking around the hall... I saw a light at the end of the hall and people wearing black are walking towards me.

They stood right in front of me.

"Hi Anna" the man in the middle said. I don't know who they are. They look like they will murder someone.

"Do you have a good time with them Anna? The man in the middle asks again. With who? Lucas and Marcus? I wonder where is the both of them. Did they leave me here?

"Untie her Boys"

"Let me tell you about Lucas and Marcus, Lucas was the first born and Marcus was the second one..." What??? I thought they are best friends... I listened to this man because I was curious about their identity.

He continues "Lucas picks a girl that Marcus would get to make her fall in love when Marcus fucks her. Lucas will meet the girl and both of them will play with her. It was their play time. They are used to doing it. Then if the time is up. They'll give them to me as my sex slaves. You know why? They are my son. I am the one who teaches them." So... this is what Lucas and Marcus are talking about.

"No, I'm going. Get out of the Way!" I yelled and pushed them to move but they didn't even budge. Instead, two of his man hold onto me.

"I'll let you suffer lady" He said. It gives me shivers down to my spine. I was so scared that I started getting my arms but they are a lot stronger than me. The man in the middle slapped me hard that I started crying.. *Lucas Marcus, please come and save me from your father...*

"Call me Mr. Cronos"

Mr. Cronos started unbuttoning my sleepwear. Nearly exposing to all of them my nipples. He sucked one of my nipples and massaged the other one.

I cried loudly as he pushed two fingers in my pussy. Do I deserve this life?

"NO PLEASE DON'T DO THIS" I cried. But he doesn't listen he pushed his fingers deeper.

He takes off his pants and thrust his crotch inside me. I winced in pain. I am still not wet that's why it hurts. He thrust more and tears are rolling down on my face.

He cupped my face and slap me four times. "You're good you bitch" he said. I never thought that I would go through all of this.

"Do you want to taste him boys?" he asked them.

"Please no, I beg you let go of me please... I don't want this" I begged them. But they all laughed at me. Mr.Cronos thrusts faster and I feel like he was about to come.

"UGH please don't come inside of me" but he didn't listen he cums on my pussy. After he is finished with me. The other men gets a table.

I resist and begging them to let me go.
They all hold onto me touched my body.
My body is so tired. They all take turns
on fucking me. My pussy is now sore and
I am filled with their cums.

They all are not tired. They are enjoying
what they are doing. I can't cry anymore.
What's the use of crying? When they all
did these nasty stuffs on me. I'm so tired.
And with that I blacked out.

I woke up feeling sick, I was till at this
hall. Lying naked on this table. The men
saw that I was awake. One men gave me
water to drink. I am surrounded by them.
There is no use of escaping.

"When will you let me go?" I asked them
with my eyes still blurry. They all looked
at me with disgust and said.

"Not until we are satisfied with your
body, our boss gave you as a gift for us.
He doesn't like you because you are just a
trash woman" They are all disgusting. I
feel like I was a woman who are not
deserving to live. What did I ever do to be
in this kind of situation like this? Do I

need to satisfy them so that they can let me go?

"Can we start now? So I can go? I promise not to tell anyone about this please?" I said with a pleading eye.

One guy approached me, I let him lie down and I started going on top of him. I pushed myself down on his crotch.

"UGH" I moaned as his shaft filled my pussy. I moved upwards and downwards as fast as I could and I can see on his face that he is enjoying what I am doing. After a few thrusts he came inside me.

I can't recover yet when two guys walked near me. The other one positioned himself on my back and the other one is in front of me. They are in sync of thrusting my pussy and my mouth.

"Fuck you, you're so tight"

"Your mouth is so warm" they both said. I was not thinking about the pleasure that I was feeling. I want this to end quickly. After 10 hours on continuing pleasuring them they are all knocked out even though I can't walk properly I still managed to escape this hell. I have nowhere to go. I can't go back to Marcus's house they don't care about me. They don't even look after me when they just tossed me like I was a fucking doll. I will make sure that they are going to regret what they have done to me. Mark my words.

2 years have passed.

One woman was walking through the building. Eyes are fixed on this woman. She wears a gray bodycon dress that hugs her body perfectly she pairs it with a silver heel. Her green eyes that can make every man fall in love.

As she was walking through the building, she saw two guys talking to each other while walking towards her way. When they are close to each other, the two man just looked at her and passed through her. She was shocked that they didn't even noticed her. She thought that maybe they all forgot about her existence that it never happened.

"Hi Miss Agatha" the woman said.

"Hello, where is your boss's office?" I responded.

"This way Ma'am" she guided her towards the big door on the end of the hall. As she opened the door the guy greeted her.

"Hi babe" the guy said and kissed her and she responded with his kisses. The guy's hand travels down to her butt and he squeezes it. Agatha left out a soft moan. The guy guided her on his desk and he let her sit on it. The guy removed Agatha's dress he removed his pants and thrusts his shaft on her.

"You're wet already huh?" the guy said. She moaned as the guy thrusts slowly letting her feel the pleasure.

"Yes fuck me more please Drake" she answered. Drake fucks her faster she doesn't know where to positioned her head because of the pleasure she was feeling.

Drake stops and carries her towards the bathroom. He pushed her on the sink let her face the mirror in front of her. Drake slowly pushed his shaft inside her. Agatha closes her eyes as she felt the sensation. Drake chokes her from behind.

"Look at yourself, Look at me fucking that pussy" he whispered in her ears. She looks at the mirror, Drake was looking at her intensely. Drake thrusts faster and faster. She closed her eyes and screamed Drake's name. Drake grabbed her hair.

"I SAID LOOK AT ME WHILE FUCKING YOUR PUSSY!" He shouted.

Agatha's POV

Ugh. It felt so good. I opened my eyes and looks at myself getting fucked in the mirror.

"More Drake, more" I said. He grabs my boobs and massaged it while his other hand reached for my cunt and plays with it... He is making me insane. He stops entering me and removed his shaft inside me.

"Play with yourself I want to see it" He said. I sit on the sink and opens my legs widely I inserted two of my fingers. I moaned as I continue pleasuring myself.

"Faster Agatha" He said while ejaculating himself. I finger myself faster as I was about to come when Drake removed my fingers and he lunged his crotch on my pussy.

"OH MY GOD DRAKE" I moaned. He is going faster and faster. I clung myself into him and let him carry me while he was still fucking me.

"THAT'S IT DRAKE, YOU'RE HITTING MY SPOT"

"UGH AGATHA YOU'RE SO TIGHT"

"I AM CUMMING"

"I AM CUMMING"

"AHHHHH!" I let out one loud moan when his juices and my juices filled my pussy.

We washed ourselves and talked. He sat on his chair. I sit in front of his desk. I visited him because I will ask for his favor. I need to execute my plan.

"Babe, do you remember my revenge plan?" I asked him. He is busy doing his files, he looks ate me directly in the eyes waiting for me to continue what I was saying.

"They are working here in your company and I need your help" We continued talking about my plans he smirks and agrees on my plans. He knows what I have gone through the past years.

Drake calls Lucas Cronos and Marcus Cronos to be part of the business trip in Hawaii. While we were at the private plane. Marcus is looking at me like he was scanning me. I can't let him ruin my plan. I whispered to Drake that we exchanged seats. He quickly agreed and Marcus no longer looks at me.

When we arrived at Hawaii, we drove off to Drake's private townhouse as soon as we arrived at the private townhouse. Drake's men quickly grabs Marcus and Lucas.

They started resisting but they can't fight because they are many of them and someone was holding them. They dragged them inside the townhouse.

They putted them into a chair and tied them.

"What is this Drake Montenegro?!" Lucas yelled. I smiled seeing them looked puzzled.

"Hi Boys!" I said and walked towards them. They look and watched me while I was walking. Looks like Lucas doesn't recognize me at all. Marcus was looking at me straight into my eyes. Oh boy, you knew it was me.

"WHO ARE YOU?" Lucas asked.

"Aww. You already forgot about me? After you've done fantasizing my body? Lucas looks so confused on what I am saying. Haha I am not doing anything yet. Marcus stayed quiet.

"BOYS LET THE GIRLS OUT!" I commanded. I didn't even bother listen to Lucas's questions. I am about to start. Let the game begin! This would be a fun vacation after all!

"Girls you know what to do" I said. The two girls started walking towards Lucas and Marcus.

They grabbed their crotches while they are still wearing their pants. Lucas looks so excited about this. Marcus was still quiet.

The girls begin with their play. They started pulling their pants off. Sucking their dicks. Lucas enjoys it not until it is too much huh hahaha.

"UGH"

"DO YOU LIKE IT?"

"MORE MORE"

"FUCK ME COME ON"

"DO IT FASTER"

All moans are heard from the townhouse. Drake and I silently sit on a Sala set while the girls are enjoying Drake and I kissed passionately. His hands started roaming around my body. I am heated and I want us to fuck right now. As I open my eyes it was at Marcus's place and I was shocked to see that he was looking at us. Drake's kisses travel down to my neck sucking my neck I let out a moan while looking directly at Marcus who is watching us.

We were making out in front of them but Marcus was the only one who is watching us. He doesn't mind the girl on his lap riding his crotch.

After a few more hours, Lucas is exhausted and as well as Marcus they are dripping in sweats and they are surrounded by their cums. I looked at them I stand in front of them while the girls are doing a hand job for them.

"I'm so tired, let them stop" Lucas said with a hoarse voice. I was waiting for Marcus to beg or talk but I am disappointed he doesn't even talk. He looks tired and all.

"Do you remember me now?" I asked Lucas. He slowly looked at me. He is trying his best to remember me but he failed he looked down.

"I'm sorry, I don't know you" he replied.

"Let me rewind it for you, I once lived in a peaceful life. Fulfilling my dream to become a model. But one day one guy approached me, he was sweet, kind and he was everything that I could imagined for my ideal guy but it doesn't stop there this guy introduced me to his so-called best friend. I accepted everything about them. Even though of what they did to me. I still said it to myself that I will always forgive and understand them but that fucking night after you guys fucked me! YOU JUST THROW ME AWAY LIKE I WAS A FUCKING GARBAGE! YOUR FILTHY FATHER AND HIS MEN USED ME LIKE I WAS A FUCKING SEX DOLL! I CAN'T UNDERSTAND WHY? WHY AM I THE ONE THAT IS SUFFERING? WHAT DID I DO WRONG TO ALL OF YOU?!

Lucas was shocked and Marcus was just staring at me blankly. Lucas was about to say something but Marcus interrupted him from talking.

"I am not interested at you first, they told me that you were the next target. We found out late that you are the daughter who killed our mother. That's why our father was like this. You are the last target. We are only going to let you suffer to make you feel what we have felt when we lost our mother. We don't know what happened to you after that night" Marcus said.

"I never know what happened to your Mom, My Mom is in jail so why are you taking revenge? My mom is paying for what she did to your family." I said.

"Our father wants to take revenge on you, we were just a kid back then when that happens and you are the one who saw that your mother shot Mom."

"Why didn't you even helped me when you leave me alone in that hall?"

"We are outside at that time, when we saw our father walking outside of the hall. We asked for you but our father tells us that his men would get you home. We resisted but his men knocked us out. The next thing we knew is we are at our house. We are waiting for you to come back. We looked for you but you were nowhere to be found" Lucas said.

I was holding my tears. I shake my head not believing what they are talking about. They are just saying this to make me pity

them. They can never trick me again!
Never in my life!

Drake, ordered his men to untie them and
beat them up. As I was looking at them...
is this what I wanted? Is this worth it?
Am I right on who to get revenge on? As I
was looking at Lucas and Marcus get
beaten up they didn't even fight they just
let themselves be beaten.

"STOP! EVERYBODY PLEASE STOP!" I
yelled and cried. It hurts so much but I
am not happy. 2 years living in a life full
of hatred. Planning on how to get revenge
on them. It was not worth it at all.

"Everybody rest, We'll talk about this
tomorrow" Drake said. All of them leave
the townhouse. Lucas and Marcus stayed.
Drake looked at them but the two men
are looking down.

"Get some sleep, you can sleep here with
us tonight. We have some extra room"
Drake added. Drake lifted me up and
carries me to our room. I was crying and
sobbing when Drake hugged me.

"It's okay, everything will be all right babe. I'll fight for you" I continued to cry on his shoulder and as soon as I get tired, I fall asleep.

The next following day, Drake wake me up. Asks me to get ready that they are in the kitchen getting ready for breakfast. I go down to see that Marcus and Lucas are sitting in front of Drake. The two of them are looking down. I sat on the chair beside Drake. Marcus opened his mouth but I hurriedly said.

"Let's have a peaceful breakfast first" he closes his mouth. And we all focused on eating. After we are done eating the four of us decided to talk on the living room.

I asked them what is their plan on what's happening.

"What are you going to do with your father?" I ask they didn't respond to my questions they just looked down. I can see that they have a lot of bruises in their body especially in their faces. They still kept being silent so I proceeded on talking about what's my suggestions.

"Your father committed crimes, on woman. He needs to go in jail. I want him to rot in jail and pay for his sins."

They kept silent and looks at each other. When we go back, I told them to gather information and evidence against their father. After a month or so their father hides and are not seen in this country. It was hard. I still think that maybe it was a sign for me to give up and forget about what happened and move on but Drake is really consistent on it. We have found were Mr. Cronos's whereabouts. We have filed and fight against him.

We have won against him, he was paying for his sins in jail, I didn't pressed charge on Lucas and Marcus. They are all victims too by their father. I knew they deserve to live their life fighting for their rights and happiness. They are now free from the chains that their father locked them up.

I visited my mother in Jail, she was still beautiful as ever.

"Hello Mom, how are you? I visited just to say that I will be gone for the next years. I will be living in States. I got accepted by a model agency. It was my dream job after all. Aren't you proud of me Mom?" she was still unresponsive. I know that she repents all of her sins... I hold her hand and kissed it one last time. I hugged and kissed her cheek.

I was about to leave when I hear my mom says "I am almost proud of you Anna" and tears keeps pouring down on my face. I glanced at her one last time and continues to walk away.

1 year later...

"Pose Anna"

"1,2,3, *click*"

"That's right Anna, strike a pose"

"Okay, wrap it up"

"Hi babe! I'm sorry to keep you waiting" Anna said.

"It's okay Agatha- I mean Anna. I'm still not used of calling you Anna, babe"

"Let's go home Anna"

When we got home, Drake started kissing me roughly. Oh god I missed this since when was the last, we do it. Never mind I was so overwhelmed of what we are doing right now.

His hands slide into my panty, sliding his fingers inside me...

"You're so wet huh" He chuckles while saying. I moaned as his fingers move inside me.

"Oh God Drake" he kneels in front of me.

"You're so beautiful" and he eats my pussy like he was a hungry man. He licks my cunt fast while his fingers are moving inside me. I can feel the sensation building up inside my pussy. My walls began to tighten and I know that Drake feels it so he thrusts his fingers faster.

"Fuck Drake, I'm coming!" I screamed. He removed his fingers inside me and suck the entrance of my pussy. Licking every juice that my pussy releases.

Drake unbuckle his pants; his shaft was ready to lunge inside me. He entered me slowly making me move my hips towards him. He holds my waist and guided me. His shaft dug deeper inside me and nothing can stop us from feeling the pleasure. We fucked all night until we are tired. We collapsed on each other. Drake gets something from his side table. He showed me a box slowly opened it...

"Will you marry me, Anna?"

And I said "Yes" and that's what happens to my life.

The Wife's Fantasy

If there ever was a definition for an ideal couple, Mary and John fit right into it. They were high school sweethearts; they got married as soon as college ended. And now, they were living in one of the most gorgeous houses on Long Island. Life had turned out beautiful for them. Mary became a teacher and John went on to become an investment banker. But, most importantly they were madly in love with each other. It would seem that they were living the perfect life. Well, not quite.

Fast forward to five years after they got married on the serene beach of Long Island, everything looks completely normal on the outside. But, on the inside, we can't even see the glimpses of the two love birds who at one point in life could not keep their hands off each other. Their busy and hectic lives had taken a toll on their love life.

John was working nonstop, which meant he could not spend time with Mary. And to talk about their sex life, there was none. John was hardly ever early from work and whenever he was home, he was tired as hell. However, Mary could not stand it anymore. She was frustrated all the time, she could not concentrate on her work and whenever she wanted love from her husband, she was denied every opportunity. She understood that he was working so much for their future, but the fact remained that she had her needs and they were not being fulfilled.

On one such night where John had come home late and slept without so much as a goodnight kiss to Mary, she furiously started writing in her diary.

"Today John was late again. I wanted to please him today which is why I wore his favorite slutty lingerie that he had got for me. But, he did not even notice." Tears trickled down her pink cheeks as she tried to stifle them so as to not wake John.

" It has been too long since we have not had sex. It seems like I have forgotten what it is like to be touched, to be felt, to be fucked. Sometimes, I just feel like I need to have just one reckless night where everything is off the table and I can have sex, just rough, hard, animalistic sex that would leave me aching for days. I love John, of course, he is the love of my life. But I never thought I would need someone else to satisfy me. Last week, I heard that some thieves had gotten into a house in the neighborhood, and along with stealing their jewelry they fucked the wife too." Just then she heard some noise and she turned around to see that it was just her husband grunting in his sleep. She kept writing on.

"Ever since I heard it, all I can think about is that I wanted to be her. I wanted to be the one who was held captive and used by someone who was not her husband. That lucky bitch. I know it is so wrong on so many levels, but it feels like that is all I ever want in my life now. I keep wondering what it would feel like to be taken by a stranger, well strangers. That lucky bitch of a wife from the neighborhood realized got to have it with two strangers. I keep imagining that it happens with me too. Somebody just breaks into my house and grabs me when I am in the shower. And then, I could have my one unhinged night with people who just want to screw me over and over again until I beg for mercy, and then do me some even after that."

She stopped writing to make sure that John was still sleeping. She lovingly watched him for a few moments and got back to her diary. "I know it is twisted, and that it will never happen. It was just a thought, but a thought that is making my loins ache even by thinking about it. Anyways, I better get back to sleep, I have a class to teach tomorrow."

And then she slept beside her husband while thinking about the crazy old days where John would have sex with her at every chance he got.

They had gone to Hawaii for their honeymoon. It was crazy hot which meant she was in a bikini most of the time. She thought that is exactly why her husband had chosen that particular destination. She did not remember seeing a lot of Hawaii, as they spent most of their time in the bedroom enjoying marital bliss. She remembered one time when they had gone out to look at the magnificent sea. John had hired a small boat so that they could go inside the ocean.

Mary had decided to wear a netted bikini which covered only the parts that were extremely essential. She was excited to see the sea, but what she was not anticipating was that she was going to have her craziest experience yet with her husband.

They were sitting face to face in the boat. They were planning to go in so deep that they were the only ones' there. The sea was a majestic blue, and the way it shone under the sunlight was simply breathtaking. "So beautiful," Mary said looking at the beauty of nature. "Yeah, so beautiful!" John said too. Mary looked around at him and saw that he was not even looking at the beach. "You did not even look at the beach," Mary said. "But, I looked at you and that is the most precious thing I have ever seen in my life," John said. Mary just smiled. It was things like these that had made her fall in love with her husband in the first place.

Just then John reached between her thighs and touched her. She gasped, "John what are you doing!" "Appreciating nature's beauty," he said, and again touched her panties. He could feel that she was wet. "So soon my love?" John said naughtily. Mary could do nothing but smile. John went down and kneeled on the boat floor so that now he was face to face with her pussy.

He moved aside what little part of the bikini was hiding her womanhood. "John stop! What are you doing someone may see us!" Mary exclaimed, trying to shut her legs closed. "Sweetheart, why do you think I brought us so deep inside the water where no one could see us?" John said, opening her legs wide so that he could get on with the task that he had in mind. And before Mary could protest anymore, he kissed her on her pussy. She bit her lip to stop a gasp from escaping. John sensing her eagerness started licking her all over her hole.

She tried so hard to stop herself, but she could not stop herself from moaning when he decided to play with her clit. Slowly he increased his pace of licking. Mary let out moans occasionally when it became too much for her. She was about to come. "Oh, John! Make me come!" she said her eyes close. If there was heaven ever it was right here. Her body shuddered violently and she came. "That is right baby! You come for me! Just like that." John said. He licked all his wife's come cum like it was the most precious thing he had ever put in his mouth.

John sat up and went back to his seat. "Come here my love." he motioned Mary to come to sit on his lap. He kissed her passionately on the mouth. Mary could feel his cock rising from under his pants. She smiled coyly at him.

She opened his zipper and made him lower his pants just enough to give his cock the access it needed. She sat facing him putting both her legs around him. She put her fingers in his mouth and wet her pussy with his saliva. Then, she inserted her husband's dick inside her hole.

She started grinding herself on her husband. It started slowly but now it was escalating to such rigor that the boat started shaking violently. She stopped and giggled while the boat stabled. Her laughter made John go crazy. He stood up and made her sit on the bench.

He started thrusting himself inside his wife with great force. Every thrust made Mary moan louder and louder. Her little biking kept coming between his shaft and her hole. John hastily removed it and he was about to throw it in the sea when she stopped him to remind him that she will need it when they were back on the land. "Very well," he said and put it in her mouth.

They both came. John kissed his wife lovingly. Now, it was her turn to please her husband. She knelt down and talk his cock in her hands. She put her spit on it and started massaging it slowly. Then to John's surprise, she put it in her mouth. It was the first time she had ever done that. Her inexperienced mouth was making him go wild. He wasn't a guy who usually made a noise, but this time it was different.

He gasped. He guided her in the right direction. And then, when he was about to come he removed his cock from his wife's mouth and let his juices cover her bikini. She knew her bikini was ruined. He splashed some water on her to wash off his juices. He kissed her passionately. "I love you so much," he said. "I know," Mary said lovingly.

She made John sit again. She sat on him facing the opposite direction. She inserted her husband inside her again and bobbed up and down to give both of them obscene amounts of pleasure.

John started caressing her breasts. He moved the bikini that covered her heavy breasts and played with her nipples. They were completely exposed to the world. But Mary did not want to stop. Just then she saw a boat that was coming in their direction. She saw that there were at least twenty people, tourists most probably, in that boat.

"John there are people coming to this side!" Mary said. She tried to get up from her husband's lap, but he did not let her go. John was having the time of his life with his beloved wife and he was not about to let a bunch of strangers ruin it for him. "I don't care!" he said. Mary could sense the urgency in his voice. And moreover, she had half-heartedly suggested that they stop this love-making session which she was also enjoying a lot.

The boat had stopped in its tracks as the helmsman was busy gawking at them. But, the couple did not care. They were with each other and that is the only world they could see. Mary kept bobbing up and down while her husband was fondling her breasts.

There was something alluring about having sex in an ocean while people stared at you. They were close to an orgasm. They both kept saying each other's names until they came. Mary knew she was going to remember this day for the rest of her life.

Just thinking about the past had aroused Mary. She was wet and she wanted to wake up John and just make him fuck her then and there. But, she knew that she could not wake him up as he had an important meeting the next day that was very important for her husband. So, she decided to take matters into her own hands.

She quietly removed her panties and touched herself down there. It felt so good to be touched there. She had forgotten what it was like to feel the tingling sensation. She started pleasuring herself. Her breathing became ragged, she was about to moan when she realized her husband was sleeping next to her.

She put her other hand which was not caressing her pussy on her mouth to stop herself from screaming. It partially worked. She let out muffled moans which she tried to unsuccessfully stop by biting her lip. She looked over at her husband to see if it had awakened him. She was half-hoping it had. But to her dismay, he was still sleeping like a log. She was very hurt, but right now she could not concentrate on any of it as her right hand was forcing her to focus on the magic it was doing for her.

While masturbating, all she could think about was their crazy day on the beach. She missed it terribly and wanted those days to come back. And while thinking about her husband she climaxed. She soaked in the bliss for a while and then began to fall asleep.

She was so peacefully asleep that she did not even realize that she had forgotten her diary on the table in front of their bed.

As soon as the sun was up, Mary woke up and went straight into the shower. She had all but forgotten her activities of the previous night. John woke up too and remembered that he had an important business meeting today. He hastily got up from his bed and swept his jet black hair that covered his eyes while looking for the file that contained all the details for today's meeting that he was going to be attending.

He went near the table to see if he had kept it there. And there it was, the file that he had been looking for. He quickly opened it and started reading when his eyes fell upon a brown leather book which was lying near the file. He knew it was his wife's diary. And when he was about to call her and tell her that he had found it lying there, it slipped from his hands and fell on the marble floor. He was about to keep it back when he read his name in it.

Curiosity got the better of him and he started reading his wife's personal diary. Moreover, he had found her recent record in it, the one that she had written the previous night. As he was reading it he fell into the chair nearby as his legs had given up. He was shattered to the core. He hadn't realized that his wife was so unhappy in the marriage. He vowed to be a better husband for her, but before that, he had to make up for all the past mistakes. He decided that he is going to make his wife's fantasy come true.

That day, John left his house with a resolution in his mind to set things right for his wife. And for that, he had to make some calls and find two people who would break into his house and force themselves on his hot wife for her happiness and satisfaction.

A week later, John had come home from work earlier than usual. Mary was cooking in the kitchen. She looked happier today, he noticed that she had chosen to wear the black lacy bra that she knew made him go crazy. And underneath her short skirt, he could bet all his money, he knew she was wearing the black crotch less panties he had got her. He knew full well that she was planning on making love to her husband. But, John had something else on his mind, for today was the day that he was finally going to make his wife's fetish come true.

"Honey, dinner's ready" Mary called out to him bringing him back to reality. "I am coming sweetheart," John called after her. He could not take his eyes off her long black curly hair that was bouncing above her perfect booty while she walked to the dining room. He felt sorry that he had failed as her husband to take care of her needs but he knew that he was going to compensate for it today.

He was a little hesitant and did not know how things were going to go down, but he was sure of one thing. He was going to do it for his wife, whom he loved more than anything in the world. They finished their dinner. John did not even pay attention to what he was eating, his mind was elsewhere. He was busy imagining what it would feel like to know that some other man was going to be bedding his ravishingly sexy wife tonight.

As clockwork, Mary went for her evening bath. She removed her alluring panties and bra and turned on the shower. The water was not so warm that it was scalding, but it was definitely warm enough to make her nipples tighten. She started soaping her perfect 5'5" body. She hadn't missed that her husband could not take his eyes off her today. Point one for the lacy bra and crotchless panties she thought. And smiling to herself in anticipation, she finished her bath.

She dried her body and put on the clothes that made her husband go wild. To make things even more interesting she decided that she would wear just that and put a robe over it. "John is one hell of a lucky man." she thought to herself. That is when she heard a noise downstairs. It was the noise of a window cracking. She hurriedly put on the robe and went on to see what was happening when to her horror she saw two thieves holding a knife to her husband's throat.

"John!" she screamed. She could not believe her eyes. She was half expecting that this was a nightmare and she would wake up any minute now. But, just then one of the thieves who was the more muscular of the both of them said, "My my! What do we have here?! I Wasn't expecting to see a beauty like you here!" His voice was even more threatening than his body. And the way he said it made a shiver go down her spine.

"Please don't hurt him! Please leave us alone! You can take whatever you want, we won't say anything to anyone!" said Mary, scared for her husband's life. "Oh we will have whatever we want don't you worry about that baby!" said the huge man. The malice and hunger in his voice were evident. Just as she moved forward the thieve that was holding the knife to John's throat inched it just a little bit more. Now, even one small movement and John was going to be hurt.

She couldn't make out what they looked like as they were wearing masks over their faces, but she could see that a grin was forming on the man's face. He said, "Now, now, if you want to see your husband alive you are going to do whatever we say." "I will do whatever you say just leave my husband alone!" Mary begged. And just as she knelt down to beg, her luscious breasts started peeking out of her robe that could barely contain her huge bosom.

" We are in for a treat tonight!" said the man. He inched closer to her and slid his hands inside her robe to touch her breasts. Her whole body trembled at his touch. She expected it to be out of fear, but it wasn't that. She was feeling an odd sense of anticipation right now. She felt disgusted by her own thoughts and started to run away from him upstairs, into the bedroom. He yanked at her long curly hair and stopped her dead in her tracks. "Not so fast babe! But I like what you are thinking. Let's take this party in the bedroom."

Mary tried to protest but that man was too strong for her. Moreover, she was scared that if she didn't cooperate they would hurt John. She couldn't let that happen.

Once they were upstairs, the thief that had a knife on her husband started tying him up to the chair. "What are you doing? Please let him go, I will do whatever you say!" Mary said, afraid. That is when the thief spoke. And it shocked her.

It was the voice of a woman. "Relax sweet pea. It's just so that he can watch us without disturbing us," she said while removing her mask. Just as she removed her mask a jet of blonde hair fell midway to her back. Mary had not noticed before that she was a woman because she was wearing a thick jacket and she could see nothing. But now, she saw that it was a woman and a sexy one at that.

On the chair, John was just as astonished as Mary to see a girl. He was expecting two dudes to show up, but he was not anticipating a hot blonde to be present and to tie him up to a chair. He could not help but feel a little aroused. However, he had to be careful as to not let Mary see him like this, or else everything would fall apart. He pretended to be scared and kept telling them to back off and not touch his wife.

"Now what to do with you? Jack what do you think this bitch deserves?" asked the woman tauntingly. "Lisa, I think this slut needs to be treated like the whore she is." "I couldn't agree more," said Lisa. She was done tying up John and now she moved across to the bed. Jack had been holding a trembling Mary in his tanned muscular hands.

"It feels like we are disrespecting the bed by not using it," Lisa said. And then, Jack pushed Mary on the bed roughly. Mary wasn't expecting this. She let out a gasp. It wasn't because she was hurt. It was because of what that throw had done to her body.

Lisa took the knife and easily cut through the knot on the robe, and then she pushed the robe away with both her hands. Now Mary was lying on the bed, her entire body visible to the two strangers who looked like they had a lot planned for her.

Jack looked hungrily at her. The bulge in his pants was evident. He quickly removed his clothes to reveal a perfectly tanned body. His cock was finally free now and stood upright in all its glory. Mary's eyes widened when she saw the length of his cock. She had only ever been with her husband and she could not imagine it to be this big.

Jack got on top of Mary. He held both her hands and pinned them to the bed. "Lisa get the rope! This one needs to be tied up, just like her stupid husband." Jack bellowed. "Please leave her alone! Don't hurt my wife!" John screamed. That is when Lisa slapped him in the face. It was not so hard that John might actually get hurt, but it was enough to make a resounding noise. John wasn't prepared for this, but he went with the flow for the sake of his wife.

"You talk too much," Lisa said and put tape on his mouth to shut him up. Mary watched in terror. Now it was her turn to be tied up.

Lisa tied up both her hands and her legs to the four corners of the bed. Now, Mary was lying eagle-spread on the bed, helplessly looking at her captors. But, it wasn't just helplessness that was making her body tingle. There was a part of her that was secretly happy about it.

It was Jack's turn first. He jumped on her as a prey jumps on its loot. He kissed Lisa roughly on her lips while biting her lower lip. He quickly moved on to her throat where he bit her and kept sucking on the bite. Lisa was half expecting it to hurt her. But she was surprised to see that it turned her on. She could feel that she was getting wetter by the minute.

However, she half-heartedly asked him to stop while wishing that he would go on and bite her entire body. Mary was writhing under Jack but she could not move him because she was all tied up, and also she did not feel like moving him.

When Jack was done with her throat he moved on to her breasts. He quickly tore her bra away exposing her breasts. He groped her breasts tightly and then started to pinch her nipples. Her nipples perked up and became as hard as diamonds. She was biting her lip to stop herself from screaming.

Then Jack moved down to her navel when her nipples were as hard as a rock. He started licking her hungrily. At this point, Mary could not control herself, and she let out a moan.

John was looking at the entire scene. He could not understand why this was not hurting him rather than him feeling turned on about it. As Jack had moved on to her navel, Lisa crouched near Mary's head and started licking Mary's breasts while occasionally biting Mary's lips. At this point, Mary had escaped all her inhibitions and now she loved every part of what was happening to her.

Mary had never been touched like this by a woman before but now she thought that it was a colossal waste that she waited so long. In the meantime, Jack was sucking on her navel, making her go crazy. She had never had an orgasm like this before. And she came as she had come never before.

Jack touched her pussy to see that it was wet like a pool. He cupped her juices in his hand and smeared them all over her breasts. "You like that don't you, you slutty bitch!" Jack said. Lisa started licking the juices that Jack had put on her tits. "You taste delicious. Now, how about you have a taste of another woman?" she said naughtily and took off her clothes to show her heavy breasts and her perfectly toned body.

John had never been so entranced before. He could not believe that he was seeing a stranger man and a woman fuck his wife. It seemed so wrong, yet it felt so right.

Now the totally naked Lisa sat on Mary's face and said, "Now, you lick me as your life depends on it." Mary did as she was told. She was intrigued about trying out new things. The fact that somebody had broken into her house and held her husband hostage with a knife seemed like a distant memory.

As Lisa started feeling Mary's tongue do magical things to her cunt. She started cupping her huge bosoms in her tiny hands. Now Jack had sucked Mary's navel raw. He finally moved on to her pussy, it was so wet that her fluids were trickling down onto the bed. "You are liking that, aren't you bitch! Now say thank you for playing with me sir, you ungrateful cunt." Jack said while playing with her clit.

"Thank you for playing with me sir," said Mary. But then, Lisa pinched her nipples and said, "Don't you take that tongue out of my hole bitch." Mary did as she was told by her captors.

Now, Jack's dick was throbbing. He lifted Mary's hips and inserted himself in her with one hard push. Mary let out a gasp. And then Lisa slapped her for slapping. "If you stop one more time, I will make sure that your husband does not see the light of the day. Now let me hear some noises from you while you suck on my hole so that I know you are doing a good job."

Mary resumed licking the pussy of the blonde eagerly. Lisa had started to lose her mind. She couldn't keep quiet anymore and she also let out her first moan of the night. "That seems like an intense moan babe. I hope you are having fun." Jack said and kissed Lisa passionately. And then he began thrusting himself into so hard that the entire bed was shaking.

Every thrust made Mary shudder. She was completely in the control of a stranger and that thought made her even more sexed up. She furiously started licking Lisa's vagina so that Lisa shuddered and her first orgasm. The entire juice fell on Mary's face. She did not know how it would taste, but it wasn't so bad. She sucked her pussy clean.

Meanwhile, Jack was still assaulting Mary's hole. Mary knew she was close. She moaned and moaned again. "Ahh! You like that don't you! Now I want you to say master please make me come!" Mary was very near and she said with utmost urgency, "Master please make me come. I will do anything for you. Please make me come!" And just like that, with the last thrust, she came. Her entire body violently shuddered and then she lay still. She had been violated by another man, and what else, she liked it. She was in the seventh heaven. She had never felt so much pleasure in bed ever.

Meanwhile, John was helplessly watching as some random man forced himself on his wife while she enjoyed it. He wanted to feel angry or sad or any of the normal emotions, but all he could feel was hunger. He wanted to join in on the activities of the night so bad. He wanted to fuck his wife like there was no tomorrow. And he wanted to see if he could have a chance with the busty blonde who had caught his attention when she was bouncing up and down, biting her lip, on his wife's face.

Now, Jack untied Mary's hands and made her sit up. "Now I want you to worship my cock like it is the most precious thing you have ever put in your mouth. Do you understand?" "Yes sir." She said. And she started sucking on his huge shaft with lust in her eyes.

Lisa had shifted to the other end of the bed now. She sucked on Mary's pussy and played with her clitoris. She sucked on her nerve bundle, making Mary feel things she had never felt with a man. And then, Lisa put her fingers inside Mary and started fingering her hard. Mary's body welcomed her fingers. It was as if her entire body wanted to suck in all of Lisa's fingers inside it.

Meanwhile, all Jack could see was the blonde's perfect round and huge ass in front of him. He could not take it any longer. He whimpered, and he could not help but feel his cock harden. Lisa heard the whimper and turned to him. "You want this do you?" she asked. John could only nod as his mouth had been taped by her.

She walked over to him, her heavy bosom jumping at her every step. She did not untie him, but she gave his cock a way out. She opened his zipper and pushed it inside her. She kept grinding on him and his cock. John was so glad that there was a woman in the deal too. A deal that he had made with strangers so that he could please his wife.

Mary looked over to John, the thought of seeing her husband with someone else was so naughty and kinky that she was enjoying herself by seeing them while giving Jack a blowjob.

"Take it all in. Come on bitch. Take the cock in like the whore that you are." Jack said and pulled her long

black curls to make her obey him.
Mary wasn't sure that she could take
it all in, but Jack pushed his entire
cock into her mouth. She gagged
violently. However, her captor paid
no attention to her. He kept on
pushing his dick inside her mouth.

Jack spit on his cock so that she
could give him a blowjob easily.
And then he said, "Wouldn't you
drink all my juice you cunt!" Mary
said, "Yes master, I would love to
make all your juices in me." And
then Jacked came and he filled her
mouth with tangy juice. However,
she could not drink it all and some
of it flowed out of her mouth and
onto her face.

Jack spread his juices all across her face. "Now you look perfect!" He said, looking at her face covered in his semen. He tied up her hands using the cuffs that they had brought. He released her legs that were still tied to the corners of the bed. He made her stand up. Mary could barely stand. Her vagina had become so sensitive and she felt limp.

She wobbled a little when he made her walk. He pushed her roughly near the chair where her husband and Lisa were having sex in full swing. Lisa was about to come, and so was John. Jack made Mary kneel until they were done. Once Lisa was done, he said to Mary, "Why don't you go and show your stupid face to your husband? And while you are at it, get it cleaned by him."

Mary gingerly stood up and took her face near John. He looked at her covered in someone else's fluids. He was not sure if he was ready to eat something that had come from another man, but he wanted to do this for his wife. He thought that if this is going to make her happy then he is going to do it. And he did.

He licked all her face, and when it came to her lips he started kissing her. For a moment both of them had forgotten the situation that they were in and they were taken back to their honeymoon. He was wrenching Mary so hard, that they did not even feel like coming up for air. But their two masters were not going to have it. They pulled them apart.

Mary thought that they were done for the night and that the robbers will leave now. However, leaving was out of the question. The night had only just begun for Jack and Lisa.

"Now that we are done with this, you are no longer required." Lisa said so, while cleaning her hole of any juices, hers or John's. She went and got a strange looking bootle out of the duffle bag. Poured the liquid on a napkin and put it on John's mouth. "What are you doing to him? Leave him alone." said Mary shocked with the sudden turn of events. "Oh baby! Don't you worry about him. It's just that we do not need him for the rest of the festivities of the night." said Lisa cunningly.

She pulled Mary with her hair and roughly pushed her on the edge of the bed. "Come on Jack let's see if this bitch can take more of you, not that she has any choice." Lisa said playfully. This was the first time Mary truly felt terrified of being with them. Up until now she had at least thought that John was here, but now with him knocked out, she felt truly vulnerable.

Jack took her animal style. And he roughly started thrusting himself inside her, this time more viciously.

Mary let out a gasp. "That's it! You like that don't you! That's right. Moan! Scream my name! Say that I fuck you better than your goddamn husband!" "Jack! Make me come! You are fucking me better than my husband! Oh please Jack fuck me! Fuck me harder!" Mary moaned.

Jack caught Mary by her throat and pushed inside of her with all his strength. The entire bed was shaking. He could actually feel her hole was bigger than he fucked her for the first time. Her entire body was hungry for his gigantic cock. She could barely breathe. She had never been taken like this by her husband. She had never felt so much urgency in her life.

She was screaming so loudly that she was sure the neighbors would be awakened by that. It brought a naughty smile on her face which was mixed with the pleasure of being enslaved by a strong muscular man with a dick so huge. She was close to coming. "Make me come! Harder! Harder!" she screamed. "Did you forget the magic word you stupid slut!" Jack said this while slapping her hard on her ass, which instantly made her white skin go crimson red.

"Please master make me come! please!" said Mary, hoping that she could have her happy ending. But just then, Lisa interrupted Jack. "No Jack let the whore beg more! Take your cock out of her. She hasn't been punished yet." Lisa said.

Jack did as he was told. He took out his cock. It was throbbing. He was going to come too. "Now, why don't you get that in that slut's mouth? That bitch must worship you in every way." Lisa said. Mary being denied the opportunity to have her orgasm disappointed her a little but she was eager to earn it. Just then Jack pulled her face closer to him and spit in her mouth. "Now, get the spit all over my cock you fucking cunt!" he said, and forcefully shoved her face near his cock.

He made her take it all in. She horribly gagged and spluttered. "Amatuer! Here let me help you with that. Say that you need my help!" jack bellowed at her. "Master please help me worship your dick. Teach me how to pleae you." Mary said, not wanting to spoil her chances at getting more orgasms. "That is right." Jack said. He started controlling her head with his muscular hands and made sure that she took all of him each time.

The room was filled with the voice of her gagging and his balls violently dashing on her face. By then Lisa had found what she was looking for in the bag. She had a long black thick dildo in her hand. "Let's make things interesting, shall we?" she said. She and Jack tied up both her hands and legs and threw her on the bed.

They made her stand on all fours. On one side, Jack made her resume his blowjob. And on the other end, Lisa had some exciting plans for the dildo. She inserted it in Mary's butt hole. Mary was shocked. She had never done this before. She screamed a little in panic. "Haven't done this before, have you? It always feels amazing to open someone for the first time!" Lisa said. She tried to put the huge dildo in, but it wouldn't go, the hole was too small. She slapped Mary's butt cheeks. "Make it go in you bitch!" Lisa said. She roughly put her hand in Mary's mouth and gathered her saliva and put it on the entrance. "Wet this cock so that I can fuck your other hole" Lisa said. And she shoved it in her mouth. "Much better" Lisa said. "Jack you can carry on now." Lisa said. And Jack put his dick in her mouth again. Mary was very scared.

She did not know what to expect and then suddenly, it happened. Lisa had pushed it in her ass hole. It hurt her the first time and she screamed in agony. Lisa slapped her ass again. "Shut up you fucking bitch! One more sound from your mouth and I am going to make sure that your ass becomes permanently red."

And so, Lisa started fucking her from behind and Jack was having his blowjob from behind. Mary had never ever been in such a situation before. It was oddly titlating. Lisa had increased her pace now. Mary was find it hard to keep quite. And so, she screamed again. Lisa gave her a resounding slap on her butt. "You just like getting slapped don't you! How about I keep slapping your slutty ass!" said Lisa and she started slapping both her butt cheeks. By now, they were entirely red and at some places, you could even see some bleeding. But Mary did not mind at all. She liked being a whore who was being fucked by two people.

Jack was close to orgasm and he made Mary give him a handjob. "Now, ask me to spray my cum on your mouth." Jack said. "Please spray your cum on my face!" Mary said obediently. Her entire face had become red by now. Jack came and he sprayed his juices all over her face and put some on her breasts as well. He rubbed it evenly on her face and breasts. Lisa pinched her nipples from behind, giving Mary some more stimulation. She let out a gasp.

Now, Jack flipped her over and started put his middle finger in her pussy. Meanwhile, Lisa resumed violating her asshole with the dildo. Today, Mary had been fucked in all her holes and it gave her the greatest feeling in the world.

Jack was had put two more of his fingers in her hole, and he was furiously fucking her. Mary felt that she could not have anymore juices left in her but she was wrong. She came again, and she squirted out more cum than all the previous times combined. The entire bed sheet under pussy had been covered in her juices.

"We love a clean bed bitch! Now clean it up!" Lisa said and she rubbed Mary's face on her own cum and made her eat all of it. Mary was so tired. She could not go on anymore. However, her masters did not agree with her. "Please let me go! I have done everything you said!" she said, tired. "Not everything." Lisa said. She kept the dildo in Mary's ass and removed the rope that tied her legs. She took Mary's right leg in her hand and lifted it ninety degrees. Then she started scissoring with Mary. It was the first time someone had did this to her. Every time her genitals touched Lisa's she wished that they should be glued together.

While Lisa and Mary were scissoring profusely, Jack went on to play with Mary's nipples. He pinched them, licked them, bit them, slapped them, and made Mary go damn near crazy. She was biting her lips to keep herself from screaming so loud that she was sure that the entire Long Island could hear her. Her lower lip started bleeding. That is when Jack moved on to lick her face.

He licked her face raw and kissed her. Then he went on to her throat. He found the spot where he had bitten her before and started sucking on it again. Mary was writhing. She had never felt so many orgasms at a time. She did not know her body was capable of handling so much. Now, Lisa and Mary had found a rhythm and they were furiously grinding on each other.

Lisa made Mary sit up and do the hard work. Both the women were screaming. Jack decided to kiss Lisa for a while. He passionately French kissed her until it was time that both of them came on each other. "Now, lick your mistress clean," Lisa said. Mary did as she was told. Jack touched Mary's pussy and collected all the juices he could find and put them in Mary's mouth as well. She was so tired. But Jack and Lisa were not done with her yet.

By now, Jack had got his strength and he started fucking her doggy style while Lisa kept violating her asshole with the dildo that she had conveniently left in Mary's ass. Mary's knees were scraped. Her hands were tired. She was all red. Her neck had marks from when Jack and Mary were holding it. There was also the mark that Jack had left there. She knew it was going to take time for that to go away.

She begged them to stop, but they never did. They kept taking turns in fucking her mercilessly. And that is when she remembered a line from her diary. She had written that she wanted to be fucked by someone until she begged for mercy, and then she wanted them to fuck her more. She had never been so satiated all her life.

Mary was so exhausted and spent by the end of the night that she never even realized when the two of them left. In the morning, John had finally woken up. He felt a little disoriented. His head was throbbing a lot. He looked around to find his wife. And that is when he recalled the entire night.

He observed his wife and noticed how she was sprawled naked on their wedding bed. He could see the cut on her lip, the mark on her throat, her knees scraped, and her ass was still red with a few small cuts here and there.

But most importantly, he saw the smile on her sleeping face that she had. She was satisfied, finally. He was happy that he could do this for his wife. He looked at all the stains on the bedsheet and decided to wash them away before he needed them again tonight, to have sex with his wife, again.

Out of Cocoon

It was Sunday twilight and our little apartment was packed with close and cherished friends. And why not, it was the celebration of the union of two people deeply in love. It was the day when my elder brother, Vishal married his lady love– Trisha. They were seated in the middle of the hall on majestic sofas with cocktails in their hand and chattering with the guests. Around 30 people were present in the apartment and in all this hustle I was trying to maintain the food and drinks supply.

"Mira… Come here!" Trisha called me with a moving hand gesture as she wanted to introduce me to some of her guests. Trisha was wearing a grey silken saree and was looking sensuous. No wonder Vishal was so much fond of her. I moved towards her managing my curls with my right hand.

"Meet Mira, my lovely sister-in-law"
Trisha Said

I smiled and greeted the person in white shirt standing in front of me. I didn't know who he was and was exhausted to have the chit-chat. I was just standing there like a statue smiling and thinking that indeed this black bodycon dress has made me look stunning. Vishal gazed at me and identified within moments that I am tired. He came to me and muttered-

"You need to take rest... Go to your room. I will handle the rest of the party."

I nodded and left the hall.

Vishal and Trisha dated for around two years. She used to visit the apartment earlier as well but now as they were married, I had to sacrifice the big bedroom and settle with the kitchen turned into a tiny bedroom. And the hallway was transformed into a kitchen. Initially, I was not comfortable with the transition. Maybe it was not just about the big bedroom rather it was about sharing Vishal. But gradually I accepted the fact that Vishal is going to marry Trisha. Obviously, I could do this much for him. Vishal is eight years elder than me and raised me single-handedly. We lost our parents when I was ten years old and since then Vishal has been the world to me.

I reached my room and bolted the door to change the clothes. Turning on the dim light I stood in front of the mirror in my room. Completely astonished by my own reflection I stared at myself and my body curves. Thanks to Trisha that she got this dress for me. While looking at myself I tasted a strange sense of tingling in my body and a sturdy craving to touch my body. I started undressing myself in front of the mirror slowly by zipping down the dress. I caressed my breasts, grazing my fingers around my skin. I was standing there, all alone without clothes cherishing my beautiful skin.

"Who would believe this 20-year old glamour-pussy is untouched?" I spoke to myself.

Being a shy and studious girl I didn't have many friends. I preferred staying solely tangled up in my thoughts. But things were going to change and I was completely unaware of that.

***

I shared a strong connection with Trisha. Vishal had a flourishing transportation business and often spent time at his office and used to come late at night. Trisha didn't do a job as Vishal didn't favor the thought of a working wife. Well, this turned out well for me as now I had a companion to binge-watch movies.

Just a week after the wedding celebration, Vishal had to go out of town for ten days. Even my semester ended so I had a bunch of time to spend with Trisha and keep her occupied.

"Mira, would you like to have a toast?" - Trisha asked while making her breakfast

"No, I am good" – I replied while scrolling my phone

Trisha came with her plate of toast and sat on the nearby chair. Noticing a red mark near her cleavage, I landed my

hand on the red mark and asked her –
"Did you burn yourself in the kitchen?
How did this happen? Does it hurt?"

"Your brother did this to me. It is a bite of
love!" Trisha smirked at me

"Bite of love?" I was confused. "Why
would Vishal bite you?"

"Because he finds me delicious" Trisha
was giggling and relishing this
conversation. "See… Sex or should we
say making love is a sacred thing and an
ultimate way to connect with another
person. When a man makes love, he often
gets carried away and acts like an animal
which involves a lot of careless rubbing
and biting. You will understand when
you'll be touched by a man… when you'll
be fucked by a man"

It was the first time Trisha was speaking
to me about intimacy... about getting
fucked. I was sensing a bit of nervousness
and a feeling of tingling between my legs.

I didn't want to stop here as I wanted to know more. Finding the answer to my curiosities, I asked – "So when and how did this… bite of love happened?"

"Oh… this! The other night Vishal told me about his 10-day long business trip. The very notion of not getting this body for ten long days was enough to turn on his animalistic mode. He tastes so much better when he's nasty. He bites me hard and fucks me even harder. And this love bite is just an evidence of that."

The words coming out of Trisha's mouth hurled me on an imagination tour where I could portray Vishal banging Trisha. In no time my heart pace increased and I could feel a sweet pain between my legs. I crossed my legs but the feminine juices were not ready to stop and started leaking from my vagina. I gulped and started thinking of pretenses to switch the subject.

"So… what movie are we going to watch today?" – I said hurriedly to hide my arousal

"Someone is feeling flustered. Leave the movie. Let me give you a decent hair wash today. Look at your hair. You need an expert to make your hair look glossy." Trisha suggested while touching my hair.

I agreed for a hair wash. After all, who doesn't like getting pampered? I wrapped a towel around my body covering the private parts and sprawled on a chair placing my head in the basin. Trisha began washing my hair with lukewarm water followed by the utilization of Shampoo. My body was undergoing relaxation and I settled my arms on the armrest of the chair. In this passage, the towel loosened and slacked from the place where it was tucked showcasing my genitals and pubic hair.

I had never removed the bush down there till then and Trisha spotted that at first glance.

"Oohhh… someone is growing a foul beast in the nether hills"

The whimsical words of Trisha made me feel flustered and I quickly placed my palms at my down area in an attempt to camouflage my netherhair. I ventured to get up from the chair but Trisha placed her hands on my shoulders failing my attempt. She must have observed that I was not feeling comfortable. By now she had stopped giggling and came in front of me. To my surprise, she hugged and embraced me in her arms leaning over the chair which really calmed me. She came adjacent to my face and said-

"Grant me to clean off the curlies"

She said these words with so much conviction that it was improbable to say no to her. I nodded in agreement. Slowly,

Trisha pulled out the sheltered towel, and there I was completely bare and exposed in front of Trisha. Initially, I felt confused but the gentle care of Trisha made me feel relaxed. She caressed my tiny bosoms with her soft palms and slowly reached my bushy vag. I was so aroused with her touch that my juice wallet was about to burst with feminine fluids.

"I should moisten and apply conditioner here to lubricate the skin. This way you won't feel any irritation"

Trisha said these words looking deep into my eyes with utmost sincerity. When Trisha was applying the moisturizer, her fingers were touching the sideways of my sloppy jaw making it painful for me to hold my juices. She carefully cut the grass of my coochie and washed it off properly. It was the first time since I grew up that I was viewing my front bottom so clean. Trisha didn't stop there. She began applying moisturizer giving me a gentle massage. While doing so she started flickering with my clit. My vagina was about to explode.

"Mira your clit is totally aroused looking like a tiny penis and you are so wet. Did I turned on you?" Trisha looked sensuously at me while playing with my clitoris. One of her hands was tantalizing my pussy and another hand was moving gently around my tits. I was breathing heavily and wanted to be rubbed. But Trisha granted me much more than that taking me to the ninth cloud.

"AAAAAHHHHHH… Fuck me!" I started moaning as Trisha started licking my clit.

I spread my legs more far-flung giving full access to Trisha. She had the perfect lips and mouth for sensational pleasure. She put her tongue inside my vagina and began moving it in a circular motion. She was sucking all the juices and my head was filled with full of lights and tingling. She put her thumb on my clit and grabbed one of my boobs adding to the pleasure.

"Mmmmmm… Oh Yeah!" I wailed holding the chair from upwards. I was cherishing every moment of licking, rubbing, and sucking. She moved her tongue back to my clitoris fueling my body with intense pleasure. It was like warm waves crashing over me and within few moments I came to climax.

"Aaahhh… Oh, stop… please stop" I exclaimed literally begging my master. The place was filled with essence of feminine fluids. Trisha gave me the orgasm that I didn't even know existed. She gave a gentle peck on my pussy and sat on my lap.

* * *

From that day onwards a strange bond developed between me and Trisha. We were inseparable. I often reddened while listening to her endless stories holding her hand. After that episode, we didn't have any sexual encounter but even then I could sense the sensual tension between us. She used to come into my room in the noon to take a nap and cuddle me in a spoon position. Her body fragrance and magical touch were enough to drive me crazy. Every noontime Trisha joined me in my bunk and made my heart pound like a maniac. Another pounding was in the down region. To control my arousal I used to cross my legs and pretend to sleep. But in my imagination, I was doing all sorts of nasty things to Trisha. I hadn't seen her naked but there was no boundary to my thoughts.

Soon Vishal returned and Trisha got occupied with him. Still, my sweet lady managed to escape in the afternoon and accompany me in my bed. Since his return, the sounds of humping were louder in their bedroom. "When a man makes love, he often gets carried away and acts like an animal" I could hear this statement said by Trisha in my mind again and again. One distinct night the banging and moaning sounds were more turbulent than usual. As I went to the kitchen to get a glassful of water, I observed that the entrance to their bedroom was open and I could see Vishal fucking Trisha in doggy style penetrating her from backward. And Trisha appeared to relish all the spanks and groping. To be honest, the picture was so ravishing that I was turned on seeing them.

I sneaked back to my dim-lit room without making any noise and left the room open. I was all set to give a sex feast to myself and the sex sonances were going to be my helping hand. I was getting out of my clothes and to my displeasure, the moaning sounds doomed. I lied on my bed naked disappointedly. Just in few moments, Trisha was there all naked.

"Oh my my! Get your ass on my bed. I want to do bad things to you" I exclaimed looking at her beautiful curves. Her body was way more beautiful than I dreamed. Her hourglass-shaped body was dragging me towards her.

"I didn't know you would welcome me without clothes" She giggled and rested on top of me.

It was the first time that her body was so imminent to mine and I could feel her skin. I started moving my fingers around her body exploring her thighs and much more.

"I swear I won't stop today until you would plead me to" I wanted to fuck her and also get fucked. It was the fantasy that I pictured every afternoon when she clutched me and shared the bed with me. I started kissing her and caressing her neck. Trisha was mine for the night. Tonight I was going to taste her feminine liquids and suck all the juices.

"You want to fuck me, right?" Trisha asked with a hidden smile.

"Yes" I said slowly as I knew something was going on in her mind.

"Then I have a condition"

-      "What condition?"

"Taste Vishal's dick" – Trisha smirked

- "Wouldn't he wake up?"

"Don't worry honey. He is way too drunk and exhausted to experience the adventure"

Trisha wanted me to suck my brother's dick. I dissented at first but with all of her sensuous play, Trisha convinced me. I hesitantly agreed and acted as if I was bothered, but I was euphoric to feel a man's cock in my mouth. And as a reward, I was going to fuck Trisha and get the orgasm that I was craving for.

"Fine! I will suck a big penis and in return you will suck my tiny penis" – I whispered in her ears

As we went inside Vishal's room, he was lying there unclothed, uncovered and bare. Even his penis was resting in shrunken position.

"Let me show you the magic of touch" – Trisha said proudly

She settled her hand close to Vishal's penis and started stirring her fingers on his balls. She slowly rubbed his penis and awakened the phallus beast. His penis was erected and firm within a minute. It was the first time I witnessed a penis becoming stiff. Vishal groaned a little but he was deep in sleep. I was fascinated by the mystic touch that Trisha possessed. She told me to suck Vishal's dick with a hand gesture. My mouth was dry and my body was trembling with the thought of feeling a man's cock in my mouth. I licked the tip of the dick and experienced a salty taste. Vishal had a big at least 7-inch dick and I pondered that I could load that in my mouth.

I placed Vishal's dick in my mouth and was eager to savor my lollipop. Adding to my pleasure, Trisha started fingering my clitoris. The more I was sucking and making an up-down motion, the faster Trisha was fingering me harmonizing the rhythm. I got carried away with the flow and started enjoying sucking my brother's dick. It was the first dick that I ever perceived. I licked his balls and Vishal's moans were making me feel overjoyed. The long straight cock had reached at its climax. I poured his semen all over my strawberry shaped boobs. The smell of his semen hit me with sudden thigh-clenching force and filled the room with aroma.

"Now it's your turn" – I winked at Trisha, held her hand and took her to my room.

I pushed Trisha towards the bed and pounced on her like a starving beast. I clenched Trisha's bare body with my hands and squeezed my boobs on hers feeling her dark nipples touching mine. I started kissing her soft lips. I lowered down, kissing down her neck, relishing in the small noises she made. Hearing Trisha like this was pleasurable, and it made me want nothing more than to continue my actions against her body. When I lightly bit down on her neck, she made a small, garbled noise, and when I heard this, I felt the urge to continue, the urge to press forward, the urge to move on. I started to press my lips further down her body, looking at her as I did this. She seemed comfortable. Fuck, just hearing those noises was enough to drive me mad. I teased the nipples for a bit, relishing in the sounds that she made. Fuck, I was getting turned on just hearing these. I then pulled away, letting my hands trail down to the apex between her legs, touching there. When I touched that area, I watched as she writhed in pleasure, moaning at the sounds. She rubbed herself onto my hand, practically fucking as I did this.

We perched in a scissor position where our legs were crisscrossing allowing our pussies to get the most intimate and feel the warmth. My hands were exploring her toned body. I teased and bit her lower lip. Even Trisha's hands were running carelessly encircling around my vagina. I was shivering with delight. She was so exact with her touches, like she knew completely what she was doing. She then teased my nipples as she did this, causing me to let out a sudden moan of pleasure as this whole thing happened. She pressed her tongue against my lips, mingling with my own, driving me to the point of insanity.

I wanted more. I felt like I was at the mercy of this woman, and as she pressed against my clit, I fell back, letting out a small groan of pleasure. I looked at her beautiful pussy in front of me. Both of us were rubbing each other's vagina rhythmically relishing the pleasure. I made Trisha recline straight and moved my face downwards attracted by the fragrance of her fluids. I sniffed her vagina and smoothly licked over there.

"Ohhhh Mira… be my bitch and bite my vag" Trisha squealed with pleasure.

I spread her legs wide open and started sucking the delicious fluids. I licked the walls of her vags with ecstasy. Her moaning sounds were the confirmation of her pleasure. I placed my hands beneath her buttocks uplifting it from downwards and getting complete access to her pussy. I put my tongue inside her which drove her crazy.The sounds that she made were delectable, and soon, I started to move up, lightly licking her clit as I continued to tease her. She began to moan and squirm under me, and I found that to be the hottest thing ever.

I was so turned on and wanted to be licked and also enjoy the fragrance of Trisha's juices around me.

"Do you want to try Sixty-Nine?" I asked craving for it and Trisha agreed. I put my pussy on top of Trisha's mouth and started relishing the pleasuring her with my licks. But, what I didn't expect was what she did next. She did press her lips against my pussy, teasing it, but then, she slipped a finger into there, pressing into me. The sudden penetration was a bit surprising, but it felt so good.

I began to moan, immediately relishing in the touch. She thrust her finger into there, moving at a rhythmic pace, and as she continued to tease my clit as she did this, I immediately began to lose it. I started to move my fingers against there, doing the same thing to her. I slipped one in, but soon, she was so open and ready that I inserted two, all while moving my tongue in circles against her clit, relishing in the sounds. The two of us were an orchestra of moans and groans, both of us leaning against one another. It didn't take long at all for either of us to cum. It seemed like we both knew what the other one wanted, and after a few thrusts, I felt a hand against my backside, pushing me down. Soon, my pussy was completely over Trisha's face, and that, combined with the thrusts, was enough to drive me mad. I then pushed back, pushing my hand all the way in and scraping over the top of this, and soon, I came hard. I immediately tensed up, feeling every fiber in my body start to tense, and then I was able to relax. I then looked over at her, and she was in the same state. I moved off, collapsing next to Trisha and looking at her. The two of us stared at one another, knowing that this was what we wanted. It was our first time, but it felt so familiar, so nice, and in all honesty, I knew for a fact that the two of us were only just beginning our little adventure. We didn't say much for a bit, both of us just basking in the afterglow of the moment, and the pleasure that we shared.

* * *

The next morning when I woke up Trisha was not there next to me. I dressed up and went out marking Trisha occupied serving breakfast to Vishal – the man whose dick I engulfed last night. Vishal received an urgent business call and left the apartment. Taking advantage of the moment I went into the kitchen and held Trisha from backward. She smiled and wished me Good Morning.

"After such a bold and adventuresome night the morning is deemed to be good" I replied

Trisha faced towards me and petted my lips gently. She plated my breakfast and told me to have breakfast with her. How could I say no to her? While having breakfast she told me about her younger brother – Vikas and his ill wife – Daksha. His wife was suffering from cervical cancer and they wanted to consult the doctors in our town. They were visiting the city for one-week therapy and were intending to sojourn at our residence.

"Vikas and Daksha would arrive by 1 o'clock. I would be busy with them as Daksha would need me by her side. You better miss me this week." Trisha smirked while picking up her plate. The news was a bit disheartening for me. Obviously, I felt bad for Vikas and Daksha but I also felt dejected for myself as now I wouldn't get the afternoon snuggles for one week.

Vikas and Daksha arrived on time. To my shock, Vikas was the same guy to whom Trisha introduced me on her wedding night, the man in white shirt with a perfect body of model that could get any girl on her knees. That night I was so exhausted that I couldn't even remember his name and focus on the fact that Trisha was introducing me to her brother. It was a quick meeting with Vikas and Daksha as they were getting late for doctor's appointment. Trisha left with them in hurry leaving me all alone in the apartment.

Vikas is four years younger to Trisha and married Daksha last year. Just after marriage Daksha started facing some medical issues. After a thorough check-up at the hospital they came to know that Daksha is suffering from cervical cancer. It turned out that Daksha's condition was severe and she was admitted in the hospital. Things soon fell into a routine. Vikas stayed at the hospital in the night. Trisha used to leave for the hospital early morning and returned in the evening that too completely exhausted. Vikas used to leave at night and return in the morning. After finishing his breakfast he spent his time reading the newspapers, and after lunch, he dozed off. He used to sleep till late evening. In all this Vishal was way too much occupied with his business. Since I was neither studying nor working, the responsibility of the house fell on me. I had an opportunity to talk to Vikas only while serving food.

Those days made me feel very lonely. Not having Trisha nearby after getting so close to her was devastating. It made me feel like I was back in my cocoon where I was all alone. There was no one to be blamed as Daksha's condition was deteriorating day by day and Trisha had to be there to take care of her sister-in-law. Vikas also seemed tense. One day while serving food I thought of talking to him to ease his pain. That was the least that I could do to help the poor man. Vikas was sitting at dining table when I brought food for him. Vikas smiled at me as usual and I sat on the chair in front of him.

"How is Daksha now? Is there any improvement?" I asked to initiate the conversation while serving food in the plate. Vikas looked at me and shook his head with a disappointment on his face.

"Don't worry, everything will be alright."

"Nothing would be fine. Daksha's condition is deteriorating day-by-day and her body is not responding to medications"

I was shocked to hear this. It has been only one year to Daksha's and Vikas's marriage. I didn't know what I could have said to support Vikas emotionally. I just held his hand and rubbed it gently saying-

"Whatever happens… we are with you"

"You are sweet" Vikas said while smiling at me.

Chapter - 5

We had our food and then I cleared the dining table. Trisha told me that Vikas is a cinema lover just like me. That afternoon I invited Vikas to watch a movie together hoping that this would cheer him up a little. We started watching 'Kites' unaware of the fact that the movie is packed with sensual scenes. The astonishing erotic displays awakened my arousal which I tried to suppress by crossing my legs but Vikas could not do anything to pacify the tall pillar that he was carrying around. In the afternoon both of us were wearing our comfy clothes. I was in my shorts and Vikas was wearing his boxers. I could estimate the height of his penis from his erection underneath boxers which made me feel even more excited.

After an arousing scene, Vikas stood up to leave the room to hide his thrill. I snorted checking him out from the back. After a short while, I approached the bathroom. The door was closed when I walked towards it, but I didn't think much of it. I put my hand on the handle dragging it open, to see the most magnificent show of my life. Vikas was standing at the sink, ass exposed and shaving his face. From the point, I was standing at I was able to see everything, and I mean everything. From his immense shoulders to the well-defined abs lounging on his belly, I knew he was carrying heat under that shirt. There was a drop of water gliding down the middle of his body; I followed that drop all the way down to see- holy shit! His soldier was hung like a bull, the biggest I've ever seen in my life. His dick was erected between his legs, at least eight inches of meat tower. It arced slightly showing the veins straining against it.

"Would I be able to fit it inside me?" I said that plainly. I wanted to say it in my head but I said it aloud. I gazed at his dick open-mouthed for the last few seconds and saying the above-mentioned words made me feel even more embarrassed. I banged the door close and went back to my room to avoid seeing Vikas. But I couldn't stop myself from thinking all night about him and his marvelous dick.

The next morning there I was again serving breakfast to Vikas and he was pretending like nothing ever happened. Maybe it wasn't a big deal for him. As I was leaving Vikas asked me to sit and talk to him.

"Everything's okay?"

-       "I don't know whether everything's okay or not. I just felt like talking to you." Vikas said this gazing deep into my eyes and I felt compassion for him. He was going through a lot.

"You have all my attention. I wanted to ask something. You can say no if you don't want to answer. What did exactly happen to Daksha? And how you two got to know about it?"

-	"Daksha is suffering from cervical cancer which is the second most common form of cancer in women. It is treatable but Daksha's immune system is very weak. After getting married when we used to… you know make love… she felt discomfort and a strong amount of pain."

"Pain? Where?"

-	"You are a virgin so what can I tell you? You won't understand"

"Don't be hesitant. You can tell anything to Dr. Mira"

-	"When something penetrates her she feels an immense pain afterward. As in when we used to have intercourse even while having sexual intercourse she felt unbearable pelvic pain. This was wrecking our sex life so we consulted a doctor. After a thorough check-up, we got to know that she…" Vikas stopped right there. I felt regretful that I asked him such a question and made him unhappy.

"I'm so sorry"

-        "Don't be sorry. I have made my peace with it. Deep inside I know that we won't be able to save Daksha. I'm just trying to be with her in this hard time. But I am a bit tired now. I need to relax. You know I haven't had sex for the past 10 months."

I was astounded to hear this. My eyes widened right there. I was speechless and had no clue what to say. By now Vikas had finished his food and was sipping water.

"I wish I could do something for you" I said while picking the plate

-        "You can Mira. You can fit it inside" Vikas held my hand and uttered these words with a smirk look on his face.

My heart stopped beating for a moment. The touch of his hand generated an electric current in my body. I felt a euphoric pain in my pussy. Vikas pulled me holding my hand and made me sit on his lap. I was so close to him that I could feel his racing heartbeats.

"Mira… I want to fuck you since I first saw you in that black bodycon dress. I wanted to rip your dress right there and ride you like a pony there."

Putting my hand on his cheek I blushed and planted a kiss on his lips. With every breath of ours, my pussy got wetter and wetter. Moving his head to the side, his lips descended on the base of my neck while his other hand coasted inside my shirt cupping my bosom. The touch of his rough palm against my bare breast made me giddy and I swallowed a moan. He continued kissing, sucking, and biting my neckband while I just sat there quivering in his arms. He was kissing me gently exploring the insides of my mouth with his tongue. My legs turned to jelly and I would have fallen if not for Vikas's support. My stomach experienced a whirlwind when his hand started running down to my shirtwaist. My skin was on fire.

Then he clasped our kiss picking me in his arms and taking me in the bedroom. He threw me on the bed and dropped his head down to my nipple and began sucking. Yeah, that was it. I enjoyed how sensitive my nipples were and how they felt when they were sucked. Vikas ripped off my clothes making me totally exposed in front of him. I was getting wet and even Vikas felt it when he placed his fingers on my vagina. His teeth scoured my nipple and I groaned with delight in a breath and pushed his head harder into my breast.

I put my palm in his boxers to feel the erection. Holding his hot and thick penis was the first thing that I wanted to do when I saw him naked yesterday. I pulled off his boxers and started stroking his penis to my vagina. As good as it felt I wanted to take it in my wet pussy. I pulled his head off my boobs and lowered my tongue into his mouth again. Then I swept down and began stroking his penis to its full height. He stroked my boobs with his hands and I was getting hotter by the minute. When I couldn't take anymore I started screeching "Fuck me Vikas"

Vikas was playing with me. He asked one more time "Are you sure you really want it?"

At that moment I craved to feel Vikas's dick inside my pussy more than anything in this world. I surmounted on him and started nibbling his lips. Rubbing his Penis on my vagina I begged him to fuck me. His penis was thick, firm, and erect.

"You are a virgin and it would hurt a bit at first. You are so wet Mira. I am going to fuck you so hard"

His middle finger found my dripping spot and shoved his finger into part of my pussy lips. I sucked in a breath and overjoyed the moment. This was all new to me. These sensations were overwhelming taking me to another world.

"Relax. Enjoy." Whispering in my ear he employed a little more stress on my wet hub. This was the first time a man was patting me down there. And I liked it, very much.

"If you want to stop then tell me right now and I'll leave, but if we proceed, I fuck you right here"

I could witness in his eyes that he was serious and he would have hindered if I resisted. But I didn't want to stop. I was so stimulated at that moment that I could sense the pain in my center increasing by the second.

"Stop talking then and fuck me as you intend to. Ride me like a pony" He moaned when I mounted my hip to find his hard segment. His forefinger again discovered my vag. His finger propelled up and down then encompassing my pussy lips, fiddling with my clit like a pro. Now wet with my cream, he pushed his finger slowly inside me.

My vagina walls tensed around his finger and he murmured in my mouth. "Too tight.. fucking love it." He stayed kissing me while wiggling his finger to extricate me up. He went in as far as he could without bursting my hymen. He gently began massaging every part of my vagina, wheeling it in a certain circular motion, then propelling it in and out of me, thumb engaging with my clit. His mouth left mine only to land on my nipple which he suckled like a baby. He nonchalantly added another finger charmingly stretching me. "Aaaahhhh… I can't take more" I panted, not understanding if I really wanted him to stop or want more.

Snubbing my pleadings, he added an extra phalange and I cum instantly all over his fingers. My back straightened and I cried his name again and again till the ultimate wave of my orgasm finally subjugates.

"Oh Vikas… Vikas… Aaahhhh"

My nails delved into the skin of his back hugging him tightly. Still mounting me, he went to my nether region and licked the flowing juices. I swear I almost got another orgasm. I sensed his body weight on me again, severing my femora as far as he could. He started stroking his dick to my pussy to absorb the remaining juices. He placed his soldier right in front of my vagina with all the lubricants to get inside.

Slowly impelling inch by inch he broke beyond my barrier and settled completely inside me as I drove my head back at the intense pain and pleasure of having all of him in me. When I gave him a nod of assurance he commenced moving in and out. At first, he took it slow and sweet but as I spanked his ass, he got the hint. That's when he actually started fucking me.

 "Ahh.. ahh.." With his every push I screamed his name. He played with my tits and bit my neck. His hands traveled every single part of my body. He tracked my spine, his finger traversing in between the crack of my ass. I was so far gone in the pleasure that I didn't even protest when he started playing with my asshole.

I am glad he didn't go any further but put just the right amount of pressure with the tip of his little finger on the tip of my asshole that was enough to trigger my orgasm. He followed me soon after with few more thrusts of his cock. I thought he would pull out but he spilled his cum right where his dick resided - deep inside of me.

I feel the warmth of his cum inside my pussy and I sighed. This was the best orgasm of my life and I have had some good ones with Trisha. I didn't want to separate just yet so I keep my hold firm on him.

He hugged me tight against his chest and asked me to rest. I didn't even know I was extremely exhausted till he asked me to close my eyes. I felt him softening inside me and his dick slipped out slowly while the cum must have made a mess on the bed as I felt our juices slipping out of me.

I came back to consciousness when Vikas's phone started ringing. It was Trisha's call from the hospital.

"I'll be right there" Vikas talked on phone, dressed up and left in hurry.

* * *

Things changed drastically. Daksha left the world and Vikas went back to his home to perform the last rituals. I saw him leaving but couldn't find the nerve to express my feelings to him. Trisha perceived my actions and caught me in one day that I was hiding something from her. She tried talking to me but I avoided communicating with her. How could I confront her and tell her that I fucked her brother just before his wife's death?

After one week of Daksha's demise, our regular routine was back. My college was also about to start by next week. One fine noon Trisha sneaked into my room and climbed on my bed. As usual, she cuddled me from behind my back. Without wasting any moment she asked directly-

"So when did this happen between you and Vikas?"

My eyes widened hearing this and I flipped facing towards her. How did she get to know? Did Vikas talk about me? I gulped and answered stammering.

\-   "What happened?"

"Mira… my sugar pie, don't hide things from me. I noticed the hickeys on your neck the very same day. And only a starving man like Vikas could leave such intense love prints. Now answer my question."

\-   "Just before Daksha's death. His husband was fucking me when he should have been with her."

Hearing this Trisha enfolded me in her arms.

"Don't be hard on yourself. Whatever happened with Daksha was not in our control. Vikas tried to be with her and comfort her every moment. And he found his happiness in you. You did a good thing."

Trisha's words were soothing. I was no longer feeling guilty. Whatever happened between me and Vikas was supposed to happen.

"I am waiting to hear the details. Every single detail" Trisha was excited

-        "Trisha won't you feel ashamed to picture your brother having sex?"

"Why should I feel ashamed? You are the one who has sucked your own brother's magnificent dick"

Trisha giggled and her reply made me speechless. She was right. I sucked Vishal's dick and I really enjoyed that. How could I forget that?

"This reminded me of that night. The next morning when Vishal woke up, he told me that he dreamed about you. As I dug further he told me that he fantasized making love to you."

Vishal fantasized about making love to me? I always found Vishal's body attractive but never gained the guts to utter these words. Trisha further told me that she conceded every single detail to Vishal and it was like a dream come true for him.

"I have planned something for you. I will come to your room at 9 o'clock tonight and I want you to be naked. It's a surprise."

Following the command of my gorgeous lady, I wore my sexy black-colored lacy lingerie and reclined on my bed right on time. Within few moments I heard footsteps progressing my bedroom. I felt a body leaning over me but it wasn't Trisha. It was a man's body. It was Vishal's body.

As I turned to see, I found Vishal resting on my body. My eyes widened and I was about to say something but before that Vishal placed his hand on my mouth.

"Things that you did to me when I was dozed off… I want to do the same to you now"

Saying this Vishal went downward directly approaching my pussy and started licking it like an animal.

"AAAhhhhhhhh" I gasped clenching the bedsheet with my hands. I spread my legs with ecstasy and bit my lower lip with a feeling of overjoy. As I turned my face towards the door, I found Trisha standing there wearing her white lacy lingerie with an astonishing look. She was enjoying seeing me getting arousal. She moved her hand in her panties and started making an up-down motion with her finger. I was enjoying seeing her but I was too occupied feeling Vishal's tongue down there. After lubricating my cleanly shaved nether region, Vishal rose up with a full erection and ripped off my panties to make a way for his penis to reach my vagina. He rested his naked body on me.

Holding me from back, Vishal placed his penis on my core. Just one hard push of his hips and he sank his dick inside me. I shrieked his name as he moaned mine alongside me. He lingered still for a second, then his mouth landed on my neck where he snapped me before pulling away and giving another hard push. His hold on my neck became firm as he kept on giving me another hard thrust.

"Damn, you look so sexy Mira. I have jerked off several times to this image of yours like this but it does no justice to the real thing."

His words along with his muscular voice cream me even more. He kept on giving me cadenced powerful thrusts as I pushed my ass against him. His other hand came to lay flat on my abdomen. His pushes started coming harder as my pussy stretched every time to accommodate his length. Leaving my neck his hand fists my hair and pulls them, making me groan. The lights in my room were still off. Placing both of his hands beside mine he tangled them together as his speed increased.

I turned my face sideways to look at him and he tilted his neck to reach my lips. He licked my lips a few times teasing them, biting them before pulling them into a smooch then biting my jaw. My whole body started buzzing with a strong need to cum as my orgasm started building. I could hear the steady thumps of his thrusts as his balls slapping against me every time.

His one more push and I found my release. I had to bite my hand to keep from screaming or moaning out loud as pleasure rushed through my whole body. But Vishal didn't have any problem showing his pleasure out loud because he groaned too loud while spilling his cum inside me.

"Ohh yeah Mira, fuck baby. So good.. you feel so good." He kept thrusting till I felt his cock softening inside me.

I felt both of our cum running down my thighs which feel sticky. I didn't have enough energy to walk because I was totally exhausted. I heard Trisha's moans. My lady satisfied herself and within a few moments, she joined us in our bed.

After a long night of several fucks, three of us were exhausted the other morning. Vishal had to leave for work. I was lying on Trisha all messed up and was missing Vikas badly. I shared my thoughts with Trisha and she promised me that she will make some arrangements. The very next morning she called Vikas and invited him to our place.

"Threesome turned out to be good. How about foursome?" Trisha winked at me.

In the evening both men were there in the apartment. We started with food and cocktails. After a few rounds of drinks, I proposed a game.

"Let's play a game. I will switch off the lights and all of us will grab our partner. Later on, I will turn on the light" Everyone agreed as they were drunk enough to understand that the game doesn't make any sense. I winked at Trisha and she picked the signal. After switching the lights off, I pushed Trisha towards Vikas and when I turned the lights on they were making out with complete intensity. Vikas was blushing to figure out that he was making out with Trisha.

"Vikas don't you find Trisha attractive? I find it hard to take my hands off her." I said while moving towards Vishal and sat on his lap. Seeing this Vikas ripped off Trisha's top which a green signal for all of us. There we were ready for another night full of fucks.

Other Books

The Dark adversity

TORN BETWEEN LOVE AND MONEY

YOU CAN GET YOUR LIFE BACK BY RELIVING THE HELL

Mysterious Love

Drawn Apart

How Jealous Can You Get?

www.ingramcontent.com/pod-product-compliance
Lightning Source LLC
Chambersburg PA
CBHW052009150726
47999CB00004B/1586